For Tom, the sweetest
little monster in town ~ S.P-H. x

For Jason ~ A.R.

Bloomsbury Publishing, London, New Delhi, New York and Sydney

First published in Great Britain in 2014 by Bloomsbury Publishing Plc
50 Bedford Square, London, WC1B 3DP

This paperbook edition first published in 2015

A CIP catalogue record for this book is available from the British Library

ISBN 978 1 4088 3881 5 (HB)
ISBN 978 1 4088 3882 2 (PB)
ISBN 978 1 4088 7210 9 (Reduced-size PB)
ISBN 978 1 4088 4618 6 (eBook)

Printed in China by Leo Paper Products, Heshan, Guangdong

1 3 5 7 9 10 8 6 4 2

All papers used by Bloomsbury Publishing are natural, recyclable products made from
wood grown in well-managed forests. The manufacturing processes conform
to the environmental regulations of the country of origin

www.bloomsbury.com

Smriti Prasadam-Halls   Angie Rozelaar

Don't Call Me Sweet!

BLOOMSBURY

LONDON   NEW DELHI   NEW YORK   SYDNEY

I'm a giant monster,
with sharp, sharp claws.
I've got big, spiky teeth
and loud, loud roars.

RAAAAH!

Which is why I say,
to everyone I meet...
CALL ME SCARY...

...don't call me SWEET!

When I'm practising monster moves,

STOMP,

STOMP,

STOMP!

HOW TO BE SCARY

B.A. Fraid

If, by accident,
I fall into the swamp,
I'll be covered in mud
from my head to my feet....

...so call me STINKY. Don't call me SWEET!

When I make a great big mess,
cooking bug eye stew,

And my hair and tail
and claws get
splattered with goo,

Don't pat my head as I come
slipping down the street . . .

Call me
SLIMY,
don't call me
SWEET!

I'm a stinky, slimy monster,
with a scary monster face.
Look out, here I come - RAAH!
I'm ready for a chase.

I'm out to terrify anyone I meet.
So you'd better call me **SCARY**.
Don't call me . . .

EEK!

AAAAAGH! It's an ogre
and he's looking down at me!
If he catches me now,
He'll eat me for his tea.

He's massive and he's mean,
I think he weighs a tonne,
Oh no, there's nothing for it,
I think I'd better **RUN!**

"Stop!" growls the ogre.
"Now what have we here?
Why, the yummiest
looking monster
that I've seen all year.
Scary...stinky...slimy...
ooh, a tasty teatime treat.

You look just the
type of monster
that I LOVE
to EAT!"

Who me? **I** squeak politely,

Oooh, **I'M** not scary.
I'm not stinky or slimy,
or even big and hairy.

No, I'm the nicest monster that you could **EVER** meet. So please don't call me scary, because **I'm** just rather . . .

...sweet!